We Are FAMILY

by Patricia Hegarty

Illustrated by Ryan Wheatcroft

tiger tales

Wherever we are, whatever the weather,
Families always stick together.

Whenever we need them, they'll come when we call.
They're ready to catch us if ever we fall.

For Rob, Lucy, and Rosie – *my* happy family
~ P.H.

For my family, whose support has been immeasurable
~ R.W.

tiger tales
5 River Road, Suite 128, Wilton, CT 06897
Published in the United States 2017
Published in Great Britain 2017 by Caterpillar Books Ltd
Text by Patricia Hegarty
Text copyright © 2017 Caterpillar Books Ltd
Illustrations copyright © 2017 Ryan Wheatcroft
ISBN-13: 978-1-68010-054-9 • ISBN-10: 1-68010-054-8
Printed in China • CPB/1400/0595/0916
10 9 8 7 6 5 4 3 2 1
For more insight and activities, visit us at www.tigertalesbooks.com

Through thick and thin, happy and sad,
We're there for each other, in good times and bad.

Mornings are busy — we hurry about,
Rushing backward and forward, before we go out.

We might eat at the table, on our laps, or a tray,
Spending time together before starting our day.

When it's time for school, we dash out the door,
Eager to find out what the day has in store.

Our journeys are different, by bus, bike, or car,
But family is with us, wherever we are.

When we feel sick, and stay in our beds,
Family is there to soothe aching heads.

They'll comfort and nurse us and take special care,
And we'll be so thankful our loved ones are there.

We may go on vacation or have happy fun days out.
Doing things together is what family is about.

The beach, the park, the countryside, any special place —
We'll kick a ball, fly a kite, or play a game of chase.

If ever bad things happen, they happen to us all:
A fire, a flood, an illness, disappointment, or a fall.

We'll cope with it together, a family, as one,
Until the clouds have lifted and we can see the sun.

Families are loving—so strong and kind, and caring.
We're there for one another; problems are for sharing.

We handle things together, we feel each other's pain.
Family is the silver lining, the sunshine after the rain.

When the day is over, and we're tucked tight in our beds,
All kinds of happy thoughts fill our sleepy heads.

After goodnight kisses, with family all around,
We drift off to dreamland, loved, safe, and sound.

Each family is different; it may be large or small.
We may look like each other — or not alike at all.